This book belongs to

lois

Barbie
in
Misty the Magical Unicorn

Illustrations by
Christian Musselman and Lily Glass
Cover illustration by Lawrence Mann

EGMONT

EGMONT
We bring stories to life

This edition published in Great Britain 2008
by Egmont UK Limited
239 Kensington High Street, London W8 6SA

BARBIE and associated trademarks and trade dress are owned by,
and used under licence from, Mattel, Inc.
© 2008 Mattel, Inc.

1 3 5 7 9 10 8 6 4 2

Printed in China

Hello, my name is Willow and I am the Guardian of the Enchanted Forest.

This is a story about a magical unicorn who cured poor Velvet but found himself needing our help . . .

Willow was sitting under the Singing Tree, listening to its tinkly music, when Oli, the baby owl, hurtled out of the trees towards her.

"Willow, thank goodness I've found you," he hooted.

"Whatever's the matter, Oli?" Willow said.

"It's Velvet, she's sick!" Oli cried.

Willow hurried through the trees. As she came into a clearing, she saw her pet fawn Velvet curled up on a bed of bracken, looking ill.

"Poor Velvet," said Willow. "You'll feel better in the morning." She let Velvet drink spring water from her cupped hands.

That night, as Willow kept watch, Velvet tossed and turned on the bracken.

"Can't you sleep?" asked Willow, gently.

"I had a magical dream," whimpered the fawn, feverishly. "A white unicorn came out of the forest and cured me."

But when the sun peeped through the trees next morning, Velvet was no better.

"I wonder whether Velvet's dream is a clue to her cure," said Willow. "But where will we find a unicorn?"

At the Silver Stream, Willow threw a pebble into the water. The Rainbow Fish leapt out, showering sparkling droplets. "Could you tell me where to find a unicorn?" Willow asked.

"Unicorns are rarely seen, and only when the Twilight Star gleams . . . " answered the Fish. "But tonight, if you hide among the Whispering Reeds, you shall see the silvery steed."

That evening, as dusk fell, Willow and Oli hid in the reeds by the poolside.

The Twilight Star shone softly in the sky, its magical beams dancing on the rippling water.

Suddenly, a white shape flashed in and out of the dappled shade. A handsome unicorn stepped into the starlight and cantered like quicksilver through the glade.

As he stopped to drink from the crystal pool, his horn gleamed in the moonlight and his mane swirled around him like a pearly mist.

Willow knew how to summon the unicorn. She blew softly on her hunting horn. "Ta-raaaaa!"

The unicorn lifted his head to listen to the magical sound. Under the spell of the music, he trotted towards the reeds where the friends were hiding.

Willow put out her hand to stroke his milk-white coat. "Hello, I'm Willow and this is Oli, my pet owl. We want to be your friends."

"Hello, I'm Misty," whinnied the unicorn, nuzzling her hand.

Willow told Misty about poor Velvet's dream. The unicorn promised to help the fawn, if Willow kept playing her magical music.

"I'm so glad I found you," breathed Willow, leading him through the forest to Velvet.

"Velvet, wake up. Look who I've brought with me," said Willow, as the animals gathered round her.

Velvet opened her eyes sleepily to see Misty bending over her.

"You're the unicorn in my dream, aren't you?" she whimpered weakly.

"I'm Misty. I've come a long way to find you," the unicorn neighed, nuzzling the fawn gently.

"Please can you make me better?" asked Velvet.

Misty trotted around the little fawn, making a silvery circle with his magical tail.

Then, his eyes shining like stars, he breathed magic mist into her ears and touched her nose with the tip of his magical horn.

"Look," hooted Oli, "it's working!"

Soon Velvet was on her feet, trotting behind Misty.

"Thank you, Misty!" gasped Willow.

The Twilight Star flickered in the evening sky and Misty looked up at the fading light. "Twilight Hour is almost over. I must go home before my magic fades."

"Do you live far away?" Willow asked.

"I live in Moongrass Meadow where the unicorns graze," he replied. "I must get there before morning light or it'll be too late . . ."

"I'm coming with you," cried Willow, as Oli flew after her.

Willow and Oli followed Misty through the trees. The unicorn grew steadily weaker. Suddenly, he crumpled beneath a tree.

"His light is fading too," hooted Oli. The unicorn's pearly coat gleamed less brightly now.

"Tell us what to do," said Willow worriedly.

"You must go to Moongrass Meadow," whispered Misty. "Follow the moon and you will find it. Bring me some moongrass, but beware of the lovely Nightflowers – they're starry-eyed, but their scent will make you sleepy."

Misty gave Willow a magical horseshoe to protect her. Willow covered the unicorn with leaves and she and Oli began their midnight journey.

A round moon rose between the trees and Willow and Oli followed its glittering path. They travelled all night until they came to a clearing bathed in light. Milk-white unicorns swished their tails and tossed their manes as they grazed peacefully in the moonlight.

"So this is Moongrass Meadow," hooted Oli. "What's that smell? It's making me feel sleepy!"

"It must be the Nightflowers Misty warned us about!" said Willow. Thousands of starry-eyed flowers opened their petals and turned their heads, showering scented pollen into the air.

Clutching the silver horseshoe, Willow picked a bunch of moongrass. "Oli, keep your eyes open," she said to the sleepy little owl. "We must save Misty's magic!"

They hurried back through the forest. As a rosy dawn streaked the sky, they found Misty under a blanket of leaves, exactly where they'd left him.

"We've brought you some moongrass," said Willow. "We're just in time!"

The unicorn chewed the soft grass gratefully. Soon Misty's magic was restored!

"Thank you, Willow. Now I must go home," said Misty, tossing his mane.

"Thank you for curing Velvet," called Willow. "Please come back to see us very soon!"

Sure enough, Misty returned from time to time at Twilight Hour, to drink from the crystal pool and play in the dappled shadows of the forest.

Magical titles in this series:

Look out for more enchanting tales to add to your collection!